Joan Waites

A COLORFUL TAIL
Finding Monet at Giverny

Schiffer Publishing Ltd

4880 Lower Valley Road · Atglen, PA 19310

Library of Congress Control Number:
2018956669

Edited by Kim Grandizio
Designed by Brenda McCallum
Type set in Sprocket/Stanton/Taffy

ISBN: 978-0-7643-5705-3
Printed in China

Published by Schiffer Publishing, Ltd.
4880 Lower Valley Road | Atglen, PA 19310
Phone: (610) 593-1777; Fax: (610) 593-2002
E-mail: Info@schifferbooks.com | Web: www.schifferbooks.com

For our complete selection of fine books on this and related subjects, please visit our website at
www.schifferbooks.com. You may also write for a free catalog.

Schiffer Publishing's titles are available at special discounts for bulk purchases for sales promotions or
premiums. Special editions, including personalized covers, corporate imprints, and excerpts, can be created
in large quantities for special needs. For more information, contact the publisher.

We are always looking for people to write books on new and related subjects. If you have an idea
for a book, please contact us at proposals@schifferbooks.com.

Other Schiffer Books on Related Subjects:
Mr. Owliver's Magic at the Museum by Carolyn Bracken,
ISBN: 978-0-7643-5427-4

Author Note

Claude Monet
(November 14, 1840–December 5,
1926) was a French artist who lived in a
big pink house with green shutters in a village
named Giverny. The house, which still stands today,
is surrounded by a magnificent garden that he created
over the course of many years. Monet preferred to paint
outdoors. He used a style of painting where small
brushstrokes of paint are used to depict the colors and
changing light during the different hours of the day and
seasons of the year. This painting style is called
Impressionism. While foxes might have actually lived in Monet's
garden, the fox in this story is imagined. He too wants to
capture the colors and beauty of the garden where
he lives. If you look closely at the illustrations,
you will see Monet working on his canvas on many
of the pages. If you look very closely, you might
also find a little yellow butterfly that
watches the two artists as the
story unfolds.

For Author-Illustrator Pat Cummings, who knew the fox had a story to tell.
With thanks to my wonderful critique partners, authors Ann McCallum, Laura Gehl,
and Hena Khan, for their help in choosing just the right words.

In the middle of a garden,
where the poppies grew as tall as small
trees, lived a little red fox.

Each season, the fox admired the garden's colorful beauty.

In spring, delicate pink,
green, and lavender buds blossomed
in the light.

On long summer days,
the sky changed from cerulean blue
to indigo as the sun went down.

In fall, flaming orange, vibrant red, and golden yellow colors exploded in the sunshine.

But in winter,
everything was covered in white,
tucking the garden colors in for a long,
dreamy nap. "I wish the colors
could last all year,"
sighed Fox.

When spring flowers
began to bloom again, Fox had an idea.
He collected armfuls of delicate
petals and buds.

When he returned
the next morning, his colors
were gone!

As the sun grew hotter
and summer replaced spring,
Fox sat at the edge of the pond.

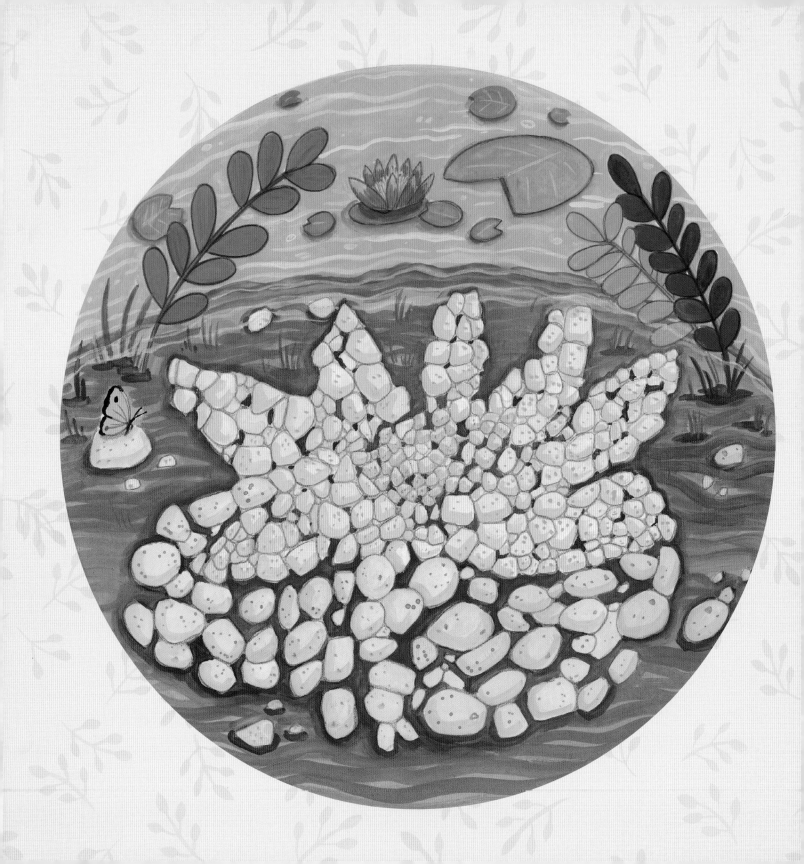

Waterlilies shimmered
in the cool cyan water. Fox collected pebbles
and placed them in the soft brown mud.

That night, a heavy rain
poured down and the pond
water rose.

When the air grew chilly
and the acorns began to drop,
Fox gathered
bunches of leaves and arranged
them on the ground.

WHOOSH! A gust of wind whipped through the trees.
The leaves scattered this way and that. Try as he might, Fox
could not capture the garden's colors and make them last.

As he trotted back to his den,
something caught his eye.

Fox watched as a man dipped
a stick with a tail into spots of color.
He wiped the colors onto a white square.
Slowly and carefully,
he added mark after mark.

When the man returned to his home,
Fox crept closer. His ears perked up. He sniffed the colors.
He pawed at the blank white square.

Suddenly, a plump
bumblebee buzzed and hummed
close to Fox's ear. WHACK! Fox's
tail swatted at the bee.

Fox's tail dotted, swished,
and swirled the colors. As the artist,
Claude Monet, looked out his window,
something caught his eye. He watched
as the fox used his paints.

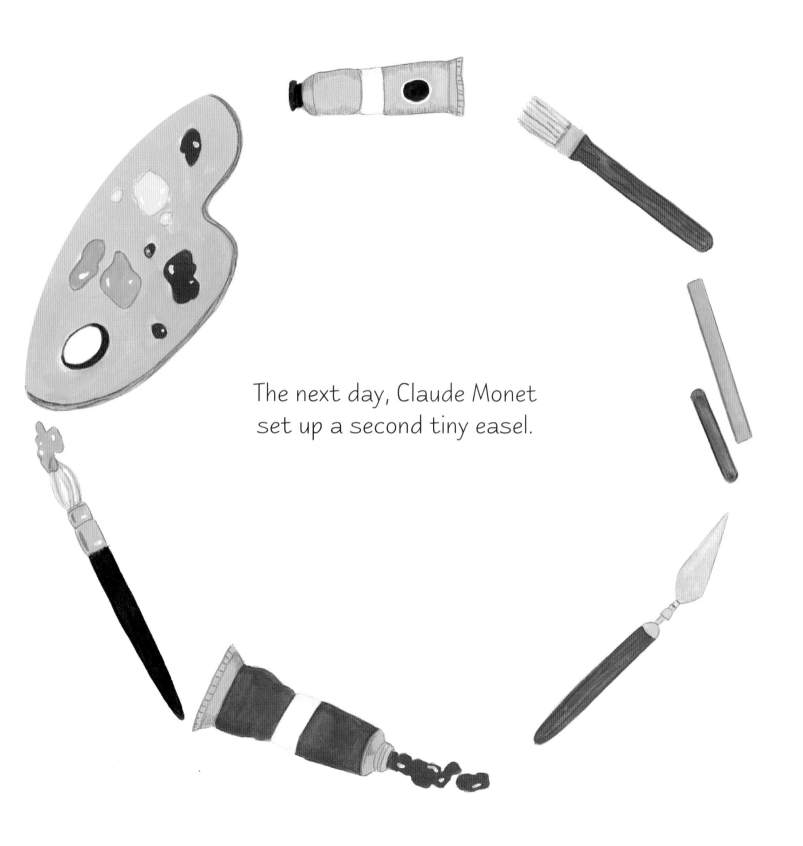

The next day, Claude Monet
set up a second tiny easel.

In the middle of a garden,
where the poppies grew as tall
as small trees, two artists painted side by
side. Fox thanked the man who taught
him how to capture the colors of the
garden and make them last . . .

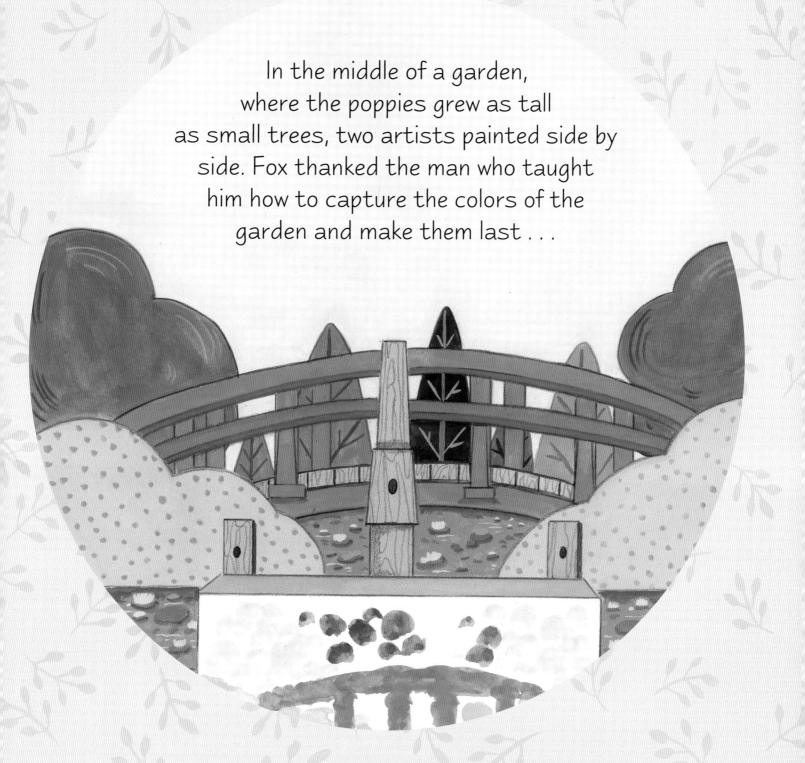

. . . even in winter.